Arms Wide Open

JULI CALDWELL

JULI CALDWELL

This novel is a work of fiction. Any resemblance to real life people or events is purely coincidental.

Copyright © 2013 ChixLit Books by Julianne Hiatt Caldwell

All rights reserved.

ISBN: 1495467317
ISBN-13: 978-1495467318

ARMS WIDE OPEN

Dedicated to the real 'Lauren' and all women who have struggled with depression and mental illness. Stay strong and know how much I admire you.

Secondary dedication to all the delightfully bizarre men who took me on dates just like some of these. Truth really is stranger than fiction.

TABLE OF CONTENTS

1	Friday Night	1
2	The Eyeball Guy	13
3	Eject! Eject!	25
4	Rico Suavé	35
5	Ex Factor	47
6	Don Juan Gone Horribly Wrong	59
7	The One	71
8	Worth the Risk	87
9	The Little Guy	95
10	Unhidden Truth	107
11	Begin Again	115

FRIDAY NIGHT

I'm lying on my couch, feet propped up on a furry red pillow at the other end. I have officially zoned out, eyes glazed over, while whatever show is on does its thing. I'm not really listening and actually don't care. Thinking too much about my life is exhausting and I'm done with it.

My roomie is on one of her 'do something and grab life by the horns' tangents again, and I'm ignoring her. Again. Yes, I know...the gospel according to Harlow decrees that I need a life. Yeah verily, even so, amen. Knowing it and having a desire to do something about it are two entirely different things.

Don't get me wrong—I adore Harlow. Best roommate ever. She pays her rent on time, doesn't steal food from my side of the fridge, and she wipes down counters like a Zippy Maids employee of the month. If I spill a little Coke on the floor, she even mops up the sticky splatters that dry everywhere and attract all the dirt I miss when I put any effort into cleaning. She graciously ignores my dirty clothes all over the bathroom floor, and she always has something fun planned.

She's the life of the party, so to speak, and I kind of won the roommate lottery when we found each other. She definitely drew the short stick in this living situation. Despite all the magnificence that is Harlow James (c'mon, the girl even has a rock star name), I have a sneaking suspicion that I have become her latest project. The lecture I'm hearing at the moment is my proof.

Harlow flicks at an invisible speck of something imperfect on her perfectly manicured nails while she avoids looking at me. Ah, here we are at her *avoid eye contact* phase of the lecture. "...but you know, Lauren, whatever. I'm done. It's your life; I can't make you go out and live it. If you want to lay on the couch in your sweats, watching reality show reruns and smelling like you're in desperate need of a shower, go for it. It doesn't hurt me any. My nostrils aren't a fan of your plan, but like I said. Whatevs."

Ouch! I watch her walk casually away, like she just innocently asked me to turn off the hall light or something. She always gets me at this last phase of the lecture: *walk away and make me think*. That shower jab kind of hurt, but as usual, she's right. I hate it when she's right. I realize she's washing dishes piled up in the sink, and that's the kicker. I have to get up. Those are *my* dishes spilling out of the sink and onto the surrounding counter. She's going for the jugular, using my guilt against me. Girl knows how to play dirty.

With a sigh, I shove myself up and don't look back, knowing I probably left a permanent impression of my lazy booty imprinted on the couch. I've been spending a lot of time there lately, basking in the glow of finally finishing grad school...and marinating in the misery that comes with the realization that I'm now unemployed and staring down the barrel of a shotgun labeled 'student loan payments.'

"You don't have to do my dishes," I tell her, grabbing a half-scrubbed pot from her soapy hands.

"It's no biggie," she says airily, trying to take it back.

I swing it out of her reach and use my hip to bump her out of the space by the sink. "Yes, it is, lying liar pants." I claim my spot in front of the sink full of greasy orange bubbles, the sad remains of my spaghetti from three nights ago. "So tell me more about this....this thing you want me to do."

Harlow dries her hands on the dish cloth hanging from the handle of our ancient oven. She turns to hop up so she's sitting on the counter, facing me as I start scouring the pot I stole from her. "Okay, so this will take one hour, total, of your life," she responds, sounding more excited than I've heard her in a while. "You know my friend from work, Michaela?"

"Friday night happy hour Michaela?" I ask, rinsing the pot and letting it drop to the dish drainer with a clatter. I grab my bacon pan from the pile and pull a face. I hate scrubbing bacon grease.

"That's the one," Harlow nods. "She started doing this a couple of months ago and she swears by it. She's met tons of great guys this way. She has a date every weekend and has ever since she started. She took her cousin Piper, who seriously has a crooked nose and a nasty snaggle tooth, and even *she's* scoring the men these days. With a face like that...can you imagine?"

"Less testimonial, more detail," I say with an eye roll. I blast the hot water and let it burn my flesh raw and red while she talks and I rinse. Its exquisite pain soothes the anxiety I feel building with every word she says.

She leans back and tilts her head up, looking thoughtful. "So we go to the coffee shop down the street and do their Friday night 5 in 5 Event. We sign up, fill out their questionnaire about stuff we like, you know, general interests, education level, what we're looking for in a relationship, stuff like that. They match us up with five different guys to spend five minutes with at the shop tonight. If we both say we like someone, as in the guy you want to get to know likes you back, the shop gives us their numbers and a coupon for half price coffee."

"I see one small problem here," I say, turning my attention to the bowls and spoons laying at the bottom of the sink now that my pans are out of the way. I frown at the mess, thinking it's entirely possible that I eat too much cereal. Then I decide a girl can never eat too much cereal as I reach for the utensil pile and start the wipe down. "I haven't filled out the questionnaire. I can't go tonight."

Harlow grins. "I filled one out for you earlier today."

I drop a handful of spoons. The racket they make as they hit the stainless steel sink, the irritating clink of metal on metal, makes my head throb. "You what?"

"I filled it out for you earlier," Harlow repeats quickly. She knows I'll yell at her if she gives me the chance to speak, so she keeps going. "We've lived together long enough that I think I know how to answer general stuff like that for you."

I bite my lip to keep from saying what I want to say, scowling a bit. I think for a few minutes and she hops down to sweep the already immaculate floor. Anger and anxiety are battling for control in my pounding head. My chest feels heavy and it's hard to catch my breath to speak. "Will I still get a coupon if no one wants me?" I ask, trying to sound like I don't care. "Pretty sure no one is gonna be asking for my number any time soon, but I should totally get a discount for trying." Like the real world version of 'A' for effort.

"You don't give yourself enough credit, Lauren," she says softly. My back is to her so I can't see her look of sympathy, but I can hear it in her voice. This makes me even madder at the whole thing. I've been demoted from pet project to charity case.

I run my fingers through my short, dyed platinum hair with a few purple streaks, currently flattened and matted against the side of my head where I've been laying for the last few days. Then I realize my hands are still greasy from pan scrubbing, and I groan before I wipe them on the seat of my baggy sweat pants. I think vaguely that when I finally get an interview I'll celebrate with a root job, and then I think maybe I should lose the purple so I look more professional...and then I get more depressed that I have zero job prospects right now and therefore no potential employers might be turned off by the purple in my hair anyway.

"You're really cute," Harlow was saying when I decide to listen to her again.

"Cute," I snap, grabbing more dishes and shoving them into the dishwasher. "Not beautiful."

"Eye of the beholder," she returns.

Jeez, sometimes I love that girl. She's too nice—like the bubble gum flavor they add to liquid meds to make it go down easier.

She takes a deep breath, as if she's deciding

whether or not to say what's on her mind. She bites her lower lip and goes for it. "Look, Lauren, we've lived together for eons in roommate time, and I've never pried. Not about that. I've seen a few guys come and go but they're never *him,* whoever *he* is. I don't know who broke your heart, or why he did it, or even if you broke his. I just know if you don't put yourself out there, you'll never get over it. So it really is up to you. Are you going to let yourself be held captive by all those bad memories you've got locked away in there? Or should I invest in an air filtration system to mask the stench of your life rotting away on my couch?"

Someone pass me the aloe. Pretty sure I just got burned.

I throw the last of the dishes I just rinsed into the prehistoric dishwasher and slam it shut. I turn to face her, folding my arms. "You're like a perfectly coifed pit bull, you know that?"

She smiles wide. "So you're in?"

My disgruntled expression makes her happy dance, because she knows she got me. She wins.

"Great! Go shower, because seriously, girl, you stink. Put on your little white sundress with your cropped denim jacket, and those awesome gladiator sandals...oh! And that little flower clip! I love that in your hair...after you wash it."

"When do we leave?"

"We can walk down in about an hour." Harlow bustles into the living room and grabs my blankets off the couch. She tosses them at me and grabs a can of air freshener, spraying every inch of the room. How subtle. "And make sure you shave your legs, Lauren. I know you dig the hippy dippy trippy look, and it works for you most of the time, but for the love, girl. Shave your legs. Most guys aren't looking for a girl with a pelt."

"Why do I even like you?" I mutter as I stalk out. I shuffle across the parquet floor to my room, dropping my pile of blankets in front of her bedroom door. Her OCD will kick in and she'll wash them for me. Even a little revenge can be satisfying.

A half hour later, I'm showered and shaved,

with lotion on my legs and a towel turban sliding off my head as I swipe on some deodorant. I rub on some tinted moisturizer, cream blush, and a hint of clear lip gloss. A little liquid liner and my industrial strength mascara work magic on my hazel eyes, making them pop. I may not be runway model gorgeous like tall, slender Harlow, with those gorgeous auburn waves of hers just begging to own a shampoo commercial, but my eyes are okay. Maybe even pretty...ish.

I let the towel turban fall to the ground, and I run my fingers through my hair. I rub a little bit of mousse into it and spray it where it stands, letting the spikes form themselves and do their own thing. I pin on that little flower clip just above my ear, a white and yellow plumeria I got on a vacation to Hawaii. My first and last vacation with...him. Before I lost it all.

I sigh. I hid out in grad school long enough. Time to start over.

Turns out starting over isn't so easy.

JULI CALDWELL

THE EYEBALL GUY

I'm sitting at a small round table, nervously picking and pulling at the card in my hand as I wait for Victim #1 to sit down across from me. At the top of the little blue card in my hand is my number: 11013. Lucky thirteen, I guess. I'm not superstitious but if I were, I would take it as a sign that tonight isn't gonna end well and get out while I can.

Five other numbers are written on my card—numbers that everyone in the room has assigned to them. If we like each other, we leave a little check mark by our numbers. It feels like an amped up version of the little notes we sent to the crush *du jour* in elementary. Do you like me? Check this box: yes, no, maybe. Even shopping for tampons on a Friday night suddenly seems more appealing than waiting for a random guy to appear and we endure five minutes of awkward silence together before scratching each other off the list and forgetting we met.

I'm startled by someone making an abrupt appearance across from me. A guy plops down and leans forward eagerly, large brown eyes almost right in my face.

"Whoa there, pony. Back it up!" I lean back as far as I can to get a good look at him. Or, at the very least, get him out of my personal space.

"Hi! My name is Kevin." His hand grasps mine, and he pumps it up and down in what just might be the world's most enthusiastic hand shake ever. Pretty sure the *Guinness Book of World Records* wants to record this one for posterity. His hands are a little clammy in his obvious—no, make that glaring—nervous excitement, but it's nothing unbearable. A few beads of sweat dot his upper lip. Kevin is just as uncomfortable as I am. This makes me feel a little better, but not much, because he won't let go of my hand.

"Hey, Kevin. I'm Lauren Br—"

He releases his eager grip and quickly moves one index finger to my lips so I can't finish. He squishes my lips to the side so the tender and sensitive flesh is jammed between my front teeth. This is awkward, and uncomfortable bordering on painful. "Ah, ah, ah! We aren't supposed to say our last names yet."

This is already the longest five minutes of my life.

"Will you please move your finger?" I ask, sounding like I'm trying to speak with my face jammed against a window. My eyes are still wide in disbelief.

He jerks his finger back and grins. "It's nice to meet you, Lauren. I wasn't sure about coming here but a friend of mine convinced me to give it a try. I mean, even if I don't find *the one* here, I decided I can make a few friends, and you can never have too many friends in this world, don't you think? I love making new friends, and I figure a guy can never have too many, especially female-type friends who can introduce me to more girls who might end up being the one. So, are we going to be friends, Lauren?"

Uh...doubtful.

I guess I hesitated too long in Kevin's world as I pondered how to politely fudge the truth, because he cocks his head to the side and makes a *tsk tsk* sound. "Do you have so many friends you can't find room in your heart for one more?"

"Sure, Kevin, I'll be your friend." I only say this because I'm not entirely convinced the guy is mentally balanced, and I don't want to be what sets off his psychotic break. Been there, done that, burned the t-shirt.

"So tell me a little bit about you," he says, lacing his fingers together and leaning forward with his chin resting on them. Normal guys don't sit like this.

I'm so much more interested in asking him a few things first. My first legitimate question would probably be along the lines of, 'did you grow up in *Mr. Rogers' Neighborhood?'* Sadly, I'm not sure he can handle my brand of honesty. Why didn't I ask him something first? Twenty bones says this guy could talk the whole five minutes without coming up for air. Now I have to be the one to actually say something. I hate this.

"I'm a student. Wait...well, not anymore. I graduated." I sigh. "You should probably know I'm really bad at talking about myself, so just jump in with questions or tell me something about yourself," I say, realizing I'm still holding my card. I look down at my first slot and see his number at the top, matching the sticker attached to his striped polo. He's not a bad looking guy, with his close cropped haircut and full lips. He just happens to look like his grandma dressed him for his first day of kindergarten. I'm tempted to look under the table to see if he's wearing white striped tube socks and Buster Brown shoes with those tan khakis, but I'm guessing I really don't want to know the answer anyway.

He leans so far forward his chin is hovering inches above the cheap linen table cloth. He reaches up and pulls back and eyebrow to point at something as he says, "Look at my eye. Do you see my eye?"

Dim ambiance lighting in the shop make it hard to see what he wants me to see. The flickering shadows cast by the faux, battery powered candles on the table are probably supposed to make it all romantic, but it's probably also to help us avoid getting too close a look at what we signed up for.

I lean forward and squint. He turns his face my way so I can get the close up, and as he does I'm treated to what looks like a collection of ruptured blood vessels attached to the outside of his eyeball. The skin around it is puffy and swollen, and the white of his eye is almost solid red.

I jerk back, hoping my lunch decides to stay put, because my stomach suddenly gurgles angrily, and what's down there is threatening to make a break for it. "Ewww! What happened?" I swallow hard and look away.

He sits back, too, apparently pleased with himself. "I have no idea. Isn't that so weird? I just woke up this morning and my eye was all red. I called my doctor first thing and got in to see her, and she said she's never see anything like it without being triggered by some massive injury, like a car accident, or a sports injury without proper protective eye wear. We talked about it 45 minutes today, and she even researched it on the web while I was there. She was very thorough." He nods in satisfaction, apparently impressed with his doctor's mad Google skills.

I raise my eyebrows. "And what was her diagnosis?" I don't really want to know, but what else can I do? I'm checking my watch every ten seconds and I still have three minutes alone with Kevin. I'm not even trying to be subtle about it anymore.

"She had no idea! She sent me home with four different kinds of eye drops that I have to take at different times of the day, and she wants me to keep a journal of all the stressors in my life. She also wants me to record how my eye reacts to the different drops. I hope it's not too serious. I have a little too much life to live and I haven't even met *the one* yet..."

The one. He keeps saying that. I'll be irate if the universe has *the one* for a whack job like Kevin the Eyeball Guy and none for me. I used to believe in all that soul mate garbage, but then real life crushed that youthful optimism out of me. I guess I'm not that old, but all the life I've lived in my 26 years has aged me. I'm a pessimist. I expect bad things to happen and I revel in saying 'I told you so' when something goes wrong. I keep hoping for a reason to be hopeful, but so far life keeps dealing me crap hands. Being jaded means I'm rarely disappointed.

I used to believe in happily ever after. For three blissful years I was convinced I'd have my own fairy tale ending. Perfect boyfriend, life on track, honor roll in college, great friends, monumental social life...and then I lost everything. It's all my fault, really. Why did I let myself believe life would ever be kind to me?

I look up at Kevin, who's still chatting animatedly. The occasional nod and closed-lip smile from me has him convinced I'm listening to every last bloomin' detail of the great eyeball saga. Part of me is jealous that he can live in such innocence. He's so carefree, like having to take eye drops is really the most pressing concern in his happy little brain. Life hasn't scared him yet with how bleak and depressing it can really be.

Wait. I think he just said something that requires a response. "Sorry, can you say that again?" I cup a hand around my ear and lean over the table. "It's so loud with everyone talking. What was that?"

He leans forward too, reaching across the table. He reaches for my hand and I pull back and swat an imaginary fly just in time to prevent him from taking them in his own. After the epic handshake, I'm not sure I'm emotionally able to deal with his hand-holding.

"Sorry, a fly is buzzing in my ear!" I'm a terrible liar, but he nods sympathetically.

"Isn't that the worst? I was just saying it would

be great if we could go somewhere quieter to spend a little more time getting to know each other better."

I've heard enough. I reach forward and smash my own index finger a little too hard against his lips. Paybacks are beautiful. "Don't say it, Kevin. We have to follow the rules."

He nods. "You're right, Lauren. What was I thinking?" Somewhere near the glass front door, a little bell rings to let me know the first five minutes are up. Hallelujah! If there's a heaven, and if that heaven has a choir, that choir is singing its angelic arse off thanking the maker that my time with Kevin is done.

"It was so great to meet you, Lauren! I'm marking you down for future contact. We need to get together again soon." With a dramatic flourish, he marks the little check box near my number that says he wants to call me in the future. He points his little golf pencil at me, and with a wink he grins, "Don't forget to mark 'yes' on 20014! I just know we're going to be great friends, and if something blossoms from there...you never know!" He winks at me before pivoting and jogging back to a corner, into the shadows of the room.

As he walks away, I tip my head to the side to check out his socks. Rainbow stripe. Even better. I grasp my own golf pencil and turn away so he can't see me marking my 'no' in the biggest, darkest X the cheap little pencil can muster. There's no way I'd consider round two with the eyeball guy, but a part of me feels guilty. Saying no to him feels an awful lot like kicking a kitten.

JULI CALDWELL

EJECT! EJECT!

I think I'm okay for a minute, and I take a deep breath. I'm drawing a deep lungful of air when it hits me. Hard. I should have known it was coming. I walk away from everyone, to the rear of the shop. I lean against the wall and shove my back against the rough texture of the bricks. I pull my denim jacket tight around me and shiver, trying hard to control the racing of my heart. I close my eyes and take more deep breaths, the only thing that will prevent me from hyperventilating. I want to go punch Harlow in the teeth for making me come, making me try something new. Sweat erupts on my forehead. It runs down my temples and races down my back in icy rivulets. I keep my eyes cinched shut and focus on relaxing my hunched shoulders and unclenching my cramped, curled toes.

I'll be okay in a minute. Deep breath in, deep breath out. I'll be okay in a minute...

They're getting ready to start round two, but I can't do it. I just can't. I run to the bathroom, thinking I should probably go ahead and puke so I have a good excuse to bail out. It won't come, so I splash my face with cold water over and over. The next four guys will have to deal with getting stood up—I'm done. I rummage in my oversize orange purse for...something. I don't know what. I'm looking for something to get my mind off my own mind. I now have a master's in psychology and I can't even figure my own brain out. How sad. If pathetic were a video game, I'd currently be reigning queen of ultimate level pro.

I toss my bag to the ground in frustration and give it a kick. It slides under the sink. I crank the vintage faucet handle to full blast and lean over as sobs make me shudder. I keep splashing water on my face so the people who wander in to fix their lip gloss and spray down stray hairs don't see what's going on.

I feel a gentle hand rubbing my back. Even with closed eyes, I know Harlow came to check on me. I turn off the faucet and look up to see her concerned smile staring at me through the mirror above the sink I've commandeered. I catch a glimpse of myself, too, and crinkle my nose in disgust. My industrial strength mascara isn't waterproof, which means I now have black streaks running down my face. No one can rock raccoon chic like me.

Harlow grins despite herself and reaches into her bag. "You'll do just about anything to get out of this, won't you?"

I smile ruefully. "Including but not limited to having a panic attack."

She hands over a travel pack of makeup remover wipes. When I take it from her, she rubs my back again in a comforting way, like my sister used to. "Sorry, sweetie. I thought you were ready to get out there and all you needed was just a little push."

I scrub the last of my mascara off my lashes before tackling the black streaks on my cheeks. I bend over the sink with my neck craned up to look at myself in the mirror. "You were right. I'm ready, and I did need a push. That doesn't mean the first time out is easy. It could have been worse. Considering my first 'date,' it's lucky I didn't puke everywhere, too."

Harlow laughs, the infectious kind that makes everyone want to laugh with her. "Speaking of first dates, mine went really well. The guy isn't really my type physically, but we...I think we connected on a deeper level."

"Not your type?" I hand back her travel wipes and retrieve my bag from its hiding place under the sink. "You mean he's not an underwear model?"

She blushes a little, like she's embarrassed. "He's an engineer."

"Whoa! I didn't see that one coming!" Harlow works in PR for publishing, and she makes her living by looking fabulous and going to swanky parties to talk potential clients into signing over rights their first born and everything they possess. In exchange she makes them rich and famous. She owns the room at these events, the kind of parties where I'm the temporary wait staff, trying not to get groped by Harlow's drunk rejects. Being fabulous is kind of her job, and the guys she dates are almost always prettier than she is. Engineers don't scream high-glam lifestyle.

I leave my bag at the sink and poke my head out, trying to spot the guy. I have him pegged right away, because he's the only guy in the room, besides the eyeball guy, who doesn't have a metro-urban-edgy look to him. He wears ironed chinos and a plaid button-down, and his shoes don't have an extended square toe box. His strawberry blond hair is receding just a bit, but his light blue eyes pop in his rosy face. He looks really nice. He is good looking for sure, but he isn't hot. Dude looks...normal. He has white picket fence and SUV in the 'burbs written all over him.

I almost don't know what to say when I close the door and turn back around. "I have to give you props. You came here to give new guys a chance, and you did. He looks like a really decent guy."

"I didn't even realize until I met him that he's exactly what I'm looking for," Harlow says. I can see it in her glittering eyes...the girl is kind of whooped already. "I'm tired of the guys who just want me because they like the package. I'm tired of guys walking out mad when they realize I want more than just a physical connection. I'm amazing, and I should be more than someone's one night stand!"

"You're totally right."

Harlow reaches into her bag and gets some lipstick out, letting that shade of red perfect for her complexion glide over her silky lips. She shoves the lid to the tube back on and drops it into her bag. "You know what the first thing he said to me was, when he sat down?" She pushes her purse strap back over her shoulder and folds her arms. She turns to face me as I rummage through my bag for my emergency cosmetics stash, trying to repair the damage I've done to my makeup job.

"What?" I ask as I reach for my tinted lip gloss, which is trying its best to avoid me by hiding at the bottom of the bag.

"He told me I have a beautiful smile. He looked me right in the eye and said he likes my smile."

"Really? Not even a quick peek at the cleavage? Shocking." Her décolletage is legendary, and all natural.

"I know, right?" She sighs, and she's looking very twitterpated. It's a dumb word but the only one that can possibly describe the dreamy gaze that's crossed her face. "I didn't even know that's what I'm looking for until he did that. Then he listened. He asked questions about what I do, what I like, what I want out of life. What I want in a relationship. He's looking for the same thing."

"I hate to be jaded here," I say as I reach into her bag. She always has mascara in there. "But is there any chance he's just playing the nice guy to get into your panties? It's happened before."

She pulls a face. "I know. But I think this guy is worth a shot. I have nothing to lose, right?" I nod, and she's silent and thoughtful for a few moments as I finish with her mascara and toss it back to her. "He's the kind of guy I'd have no problem taking home to meet the family. And did you see his hair? We'd be breeding the next generation of gingers. I would make the cutest babies with him."

Harlow James is talking family and babies. I think I should check hell's weather forecast.

I smile at her, and pull her into a hug as the little bell sounds outside to let me know it's time for round two. "Thanks for rescuing me and letting me raid your makeup stash. I think you should blow this off and go somewhere with engineer boy and get to know him better before your biological clock becomes a time bomb and explodes on you."

She bites her lip again, something she's done a lot tonight. She never acts this nervous, but it kind of humanizes her. She seems less perfect, in a good way. "You think?"

I nod. "Yes. Go somewhere far away from this

meat market and spend some time with a nice guy. After all the losers you've collected over the years, you deserve a guy who will worship you. Go have fun with...?"

"Pete."

"Go have fun with Pete." I take a deep breath.

"Why don't you come with us? You should get out of here, too. I can't believe I talked you into this."

"And ruin your first date with Mr. Right?" I shake my head. "No thanks. I'm a big girl and I hate leaving things half done. I'll finish off the night and then go pick up a pint of Ben and Jerry's on the way home to drown my sorrows with some ice cream therapy while I lament the tragic lack of decent guys in this town, since apparently you just snapped up the last good one."

"Text me if you need rescuing."

"Hey, if I can survive the eyeball guy, I can take anything."

She bursts out laughing. "There's a story here. I can't wait to hear about this one later!"

"I think Kevin goes on quite a few top ten lists of socially awkward and inappropriate behavior. I wish I'd known him six months ago. He would've made a great master's thesis."

"I'm serious, Lauren. Call me. I'll come back in sobbing that your mom just got hit by a bus and drag you out."

"I know you will. You're a good friend. Go, have fun! Go be the greatest thing that ever happened to Pete."

She's gone in a flash, all radiance and excitement as she pulls open the ladies' room door and hurries out. I follow her, watching as his face lights up at her words. He puts an arm protectively around her waist to guide her through the crowd and to the door. The people thin out as everyone finds their tables and sits down. I grasp my card in a shaking hand as I read the numbers and find my table for round two.

Game face on. Time to conquer my own anxiety, or at least kick it in the shins and then hide so it takes some time for it to find me again.

RiCO SUAVE

I don't even need to sit town at my table to know I won't like this next guy. He rests against the wooden chair, glaring disdainfully around. His back is toward me, but I can see long, thick, curly dark hair, slicked back with more gel than your average girl uses in a week. One leg is extended, one arm draped over the chair beside him as he looks around. His jeans and silky shirt probably cost more than my monthly rent.

When he turns to scan the room, I see the top buttons are left undone to show off a thin gold chain and reveal a hint of ridiculously thick, curly black chest hair. With one hand on the table his fingers drum the top impatiently. I spot a pinky ring on that hand—it's almost all I need to run out the door after Harlow.

By the time he spots me, I'm the only one left standing so he knows I'm his date for the next five minutes. He stands up, immediately turning on the charm. I'm frozen in the middle of the sea of tables and people as he approaches with a perfect, white-strip smile. He takes my hand in his and covers it with the other before leading me to our table. We sit by the front window and I can see my reflection looking timidly back at me as we take a chair. He makes me nervous. I definitely have a type. This type doesn't include guys who look like paid hitmen.

"You want a drink?" he asks me. He already has a couple of empty tumblers on our table and I'm guessing he'll be completely plastered by round five.

I see this type at the gym all the time. Well, when I bother to go. They wear tight, shiny exercise clothes and walk around like they're serious about working out, but their regimens are little more than sucking in and pumping the heavy weights when girls walk past.

"Just water, thanks."

He looked confused. "You Mormon or something?"

I decide I can't possibly take this guy seriously, so I decide to spend this round messing with his head. "No. I'm Amish." I try hard to swallow a smile. This will be fun. My heart thumps oddly as if it finally decides to slow down at the tail end of my panic attack. I've always wanted to yank someone around for fun. Maybe this will be something to cross off the bucket list.

He raises a hand and snaps his fingers at the server, who comes over with a scowl on her face. I don't blame her. Who snaps for service anymore?

"I need another, and water for the lady here." He looks at me as she leaves. "So Amish, huh? I thought you guys never left the farm, and you had to wear sunbonnets and aprons and the like." He has a hint of a downstate New York accent. Brooklyn or the Bronx, maybe?

"Maybe." I've only been to Amish country once, so I hope he doesn't take this line of questioning too much further. Aside from buggies, quilts, and suggestive town names like Virginville or Intercourse , I don't know much about them.

A look of understanding flits across his rugged face as he rubs his scratchy chin. The five o'clock shadow would be crazy sexy on another face. He just oozes smarmy charm. "Oh, yeah, *Amish in the City*. I get it. That's the deal with your hair and diamond stud in your nose."

"It's cubic zirconium, actually," I say, expecting him to flinch. He doesn't disappoint. I have him pegged for a name brander. I bet all I have to do is tell him I shop at the Goodwill and he'll suddenly vanish into the men's room for the rest of our time together. I'm tempted, but I want to mess with him a little longer. "We Amish take a vow of poverty." I don't think they actually do, but I'm having a little too much fun mocking him to his face.

"Huh. Who knew?" He looks away, and those fingers start drumming the table again.

I can't help but smile wide. He has zero interest in me now, even without the Goodwill reference. He snatches the drink our server brings us and takes a couple of gulps before I can even reach for the water glass she places before me. She offers me a look of sympathy, and I shoot her a knowing look as he sets the glass down hard and looks around.

"So, you got a name, Amish girl?"

I want to say something about how Amish don't name their children, just number them, but I probably wouldn't be able to stop laughing if I did. Instead I just say, "My name is Lauren," as I extend my hand for him to shake.

He's taking another quick swig, so he slams his cup down on the table to take my hand. This time instead of a warm hand grasp and deep, meaningful gaze, I get a quick, limp-fish handshake before he pulls back. As he does, I see a couple of rings in addition to the pinky ring. One, on his right index finger, has a diamond studded dollar sign.

"I'm Johnny."

"It's very nice to meet you, Johnny."

"So you Amish people, what do you do for fun?"

I shrug my shoulders. "Make quilts and bread. Raise chickens. Drive our buggies around." I think hard. "Farm stuff."

He nods, but his mind is already a mile away. He's leaning back in his chair in the same stance where I first saw him, leg extended, looking out the window for something better to walk by. I guess I have to take the lead for the next few minutes. "Johnny, tell me where you're from. It sounds like you're from the big city."

He grunts, not making eye contact. "The boroughs."

If I guess the wrong one, I have a feeling that might qualify me for a mob hit in his eyes. "I can't tell where you're from. Help a girl out?"

"I grew up under the el train in Queens," he says, eyes flickering at me. "My family made good and we moved out this way." Maybe he's decided

I'm odd enough to warrant some attention. Maybe he expects all women to be overcome with a desire to run their fingers through those manly chest curls. *Ick.* The thought makes me shudder a bit.

"And what do you do? Are you a mafia hit man or something?"

He smiles like he can't believe I'm for real. No worries, dude. I'm not.

"Maybe I am," he says. He leans forward to check me out. "You into bad boys?"

I look down, trying to act coy and demure. Even in real life, I don't play with players. I bat my eyelashes and shake my head at him. "Bad boys burn in hell." I can't figure out what made him change his mind, but now I'm getting a serious creeper vibe from him.

He looks away with a cocky grin. "But they have fun on the way down, if you know what I'm sayin'." He looks back and starts working me over with those shiny black eyes. As he looks at me, that old saying, 'undressing me with his eyes' pops into my head. I feel like that, but instead of undressing me slowly, he's ripping things off and throwing them around so they get tossed out the window or caught on the ceiling fan. I swallow my disgust and continue to smile sweetly at him as he continues. "So you Amish girls, how naughty are you?"

"If you're implying what I think you are, Johnny, shame on you." I purse my lips. "We take our virginity with us to the grave."

He snorts. "No, you don't."

"Of course we do. Why would I lie about something like that?"

"Where do Amish babies come from then?" he demands, grabbing his drink and gulping. His poor liver. I try to hide my growing dislike for him.

"We breed more than cattle in those barns, Johnny."

A look of total incredulity crosses his face. "That's messed up."

"We like to keep our fertility technology to ourselves," I say with a sense of superiority.

A look of anger crosses his face. "You've been messing with me the whole time."

"Yeah, I have. I couldn't help it." I don't know what I'm doing. I'm never this ballsy, but it feels kind of incredible. Maybe the emotional pendulum is swinging the other way for me now. Later the fallout will be ugly, but right now I'm working it. "I saw you sitting here in your overpriced, starched jeans and silk shirt, wearing more product in your hair than an 80's soap opera diva, with your jewelry and your swagitude, working on your third drink of the night. Who wants to get sloshed in a coffee shop anyway? I didn't even know you could get boozed here. I could tell from the moment I laid eyes on you that you weren't going to be my type, and I have absolutely no desire to be yours, so why not have a little fun?"

He thinks for a minute. Suddenly he cracks a wide smile and starts to laugh. I'm dumbfounded.

"You." He sits back, chair creaking under his weight, and looks at me with appreciation. He points at me and shakes his head. "You're funny. I like you." He wags a finger at me as he polishes off drink number three, shaking his head again as he chugs. He drops the glass, wipes his mouth with a thick hand, and snaps for number four. "You had me going there for a minute, Amish girl. Is your name really Lauren or did you make that up, too?"

"That's my real name."

"You a stand up comedienne or something?"

"No. I'm currently unemployed."

He sits forward and reaches into his back pocket for his wallet. He flips it open, and I can see the high quality black leather is jammed full with big bills. He pulls out a card. "I like you," he repeats as he hands it to me. It's his business card, black and glossy on heavy card stock. "You have a hard time finding work, you come see me. My family owns the horse track and some stables. We like cute young things like you to serve in the boxes during the races. We have high end clients who come in with a lot of cash using those boxes. When they win big, they tip big."

Now I'm mad. "I have a master's degree and you think I'm dying to schlepp drinks for wankers like you and your buddies?" I instantly regret my slip of the tongue. Rent is due in a couple of weeks and I've been spending my valuable job hunting time leaving a permanent butt imprint on the couch. He doesn't seem bothered by what I just said, though.

He laughs at me instead.

The bell rings as drink number four arrives, and he takes it from the tray as he stands to go. He tosses a couple of twenties on the table to thank the server for her trouble and shrugs. "It's honest work for honest pay. Shrinks don't make much money, you know what I'm sayin'? I'm serious—this is a standing offer. Give me a call if you need some quick cash. You need rent money, I'll work you. You want to go shopping for some decent clothes, I'll work you." He leans forward to kiss me on both cheeks. "Thanks for the laugh, sugar."

I look down at my clothes. I'm not sure if being insulted should win out over being thankful for a gig that'll pay rent until I get a real job. I bury my face in my hands, shaking my head. Commence headache now.

JULI CALDWELL

EX FACTOR

I watch mafia boy stride purposefully away. He meets another friend in a corner. Their heads tip close so Johnny can tell him something, and they both turn to look at me. Pretty sure I just won freak show of the night award. I smile and do a little tap dance for their benefit, finishing with raised arms and jazz hands. They laugh as I turn away.

The front door jingles as an entering couple jerks it open. They come to a surprised halt when they see the room jam packed with minglers holding color coded cards in their hands like I do. Since I'm closest to the door, plotting my escape by jumping through the front window, the woman turns to me and says, "Excuse me, but do you know what's going on here? Why is it so crowded?"

Our eyes meet, and recognition registers. "Holy stinkin'... Erica, what are you doing here?"

"Lauren!"

We hug, acting much more like friends than we ever did when we were in grad school. We had a few classes together and did study groups occasionally. It's not like we were besties or anything, but the coffee shop is loud and noisy, and I feel overwhelmed when I stop to think about what I'm doing. Seeing a familiar face feels like salvation.

She nudges the man next to her, and he turns. "Jeremy, look who it is!" Shock registers on his face, probably the same moment utter confusion crosses mine. Erica just walked into my worst nightmare with the guy I dumped a few weeks ago and haven't seen since.

I plaster a bright smile on my face and reach out to hug him, too. "Jeremy, it's great to see you. How have you been?"

He's looking a little awkward, and I can see in my head how the whole thing panned out. I told him I needed space before finals and she swooped in. She's wanted him since I met her. Most of the girls in my program did. We had five women for every guy, and a few of those guys were only into each other. Jeremy is good looking, the token straight guy with little to no emotional baggage, so he was a hot property from day one.

He probably only wanted me because I had zero interest in him. Some guys are all about the hunt, and Jeremy was no exception. He chased me for about a year before I let him catch me, when I was finally ready to feel something other than hurt. Erica always had it pretty bad for him and I'm sure as soon as she knew we were over, she moved in for the kill.

I want to show him I am totally okay with this development without having that first, awkward, post-breakup convo. I look in his eyes, where I still see the pain I caused him when I told him thanks for the great time but I'm ready to move on. With a little bit of a jolt, I realize I broke his heart. That's never what I intended, but I should've listened to him. He told me from the start he was ready for something serious. How come I never listened? I'm starting to get mad at myself for being so selfish, for hurting him, for leading him on.

I move a step back so I can check them out together. She takes his hand in hers and lifts her chin just a touch, with a hint of defiance, marking her territory like a dog whizzing on a fire hydrant. I smile, and I have to try hard not to laugh. Honey, I'm not fighting you for my bounce back guy.

"You two look great together. Seriously, how long has this been going on?"

Jeremy looks down, that adorable crooked smile gracing his stubbled chin. He looks particularly hot in some loose jeans and a tee shirt that clings to his chest and biceps. His curls are getting a little long on top, sort of perfect for a girl to run her fingers through. He always was a sexy beast. He rubs his chin and looks away, and then back at her. I've made him uncomfortable.

"Uh, not too long after..." His voice trails off.

"After you two broke things off," Erica says, apparently deciding to get the worst over with, "he called me for sympathy and we started talking things out. I tried to help him move on, embrace the good in his life, and move forward. It started with a coffee and Danish here, so we decided this would be our Friday night thing. After dinner, we come back where it all began." She grins.

I can't help but smile. She's so whipped. She stands tall and proud, lightly caressing his forearm while we talk. His body language is totally off. He looks around the room, shifting his weight from one foot to the next. I can see he's a little embarrassed by her romantic proclamation, and in a few months he'll have to confess that she was the rebound girl. He'll have the same conversation with her that I had to have with him.

"This is great," I say sincerely. "Congratulations."

"Erica, I'm going to hit up the barista and get

our order to go. It's nuts in here." He walks away, shouldering sideways to get through the crowd. People start to settle down at different tables, getting ready for round three. The room starts to clear out a little and I have more standing room. Breathing becomes a little easier when I can reclaim a little personal space.

"So what's going on?" Erica notices people pairing off, two by two like animals to the ark.

"It's like a speed dating kind of thing," I say as casually as I can.

She raises her eyebrows. They're painted a rich brown and plucked to perfection, a stark contrast to her fair skin and wavy blonde hair. "Really? Since you told Jeremy you weren't looking for a relationship I'm kind of surprised to see you doing something like this. You really tore him up, you know."

Yeah. I picked that up just now, thanks.

"I probably should have been more honest with him from the start," I tell her, knowing everything I say will be rehashed between the two of them and discussed in great detail with her friends tomorrow over lunch. That's how she rolls. "I knew he wanted something more, something lasting, and I never did. He's a great guy, and we had fun. It wasn't fair for me to use him like that. He deserves someone like you, someone who really wants to be with him long term."

She looks surprised, but I hope she picks up that I mean every word. "So you're really okay with this? You're not throwing on a happy face for his benefit?"

"Erica, he was never more than a rebound guy to me. He couldn't have been a better or nicer one, but that's all it ever was on my end." I look down. The honesty feels cathartic, a sweet release, so I keep going. "I never told him about..." I think, trying to find the right words. "I never told him everything. He was an escape. I went through hell and back a few times before I started grad school, hoping for a fresh start. He was what I needed to move on from all the pain of my past. When I was with him, I wasn't much more than a student and

Jeremy's girlfriend. I just needed to forget, try to live again, and he helped me. I'll always be thankful for that, even though he has no idea he helped."

She looks like she doesn't know what to say, so I keep going while the wheels in her brain start cranking. "I'm here tonight for one reason only: my roommate dragged me here, and then promptly met a great guy and ditched me. I decided to stay the rest of the night and follow through as part of moving forward without using anyone else as a crutch. When I see her later, I'm probably going to beat her senseless, but since she met someone she really likes, she'll die happy."

She nods, clamping her lips together and working them as if she's spreading out lipstick. Jeremy returns with two covered paper mugs in a cup holder, and a bag with the top rolled down and folded. "That was fast," she says, taking the bag from him.

He nods. "Tons of people here, but no one's buying coffee. What's going on?"

"Harlow dragged me to their 5 in 5 blind date

thing and then bailed on me." I shrug. I'm starting to wonder about my resolve to stay and finish. I feel like a martyr, as if I'm only here to have something to hold against Harlow later. I've scored seriously odd companions for the night and I don't know if I can handle it if things get any weirder. I don't do people and crowds well, and the emotional turmoil I find myself in since running into Jeremy threatens to knock me over and drag me down.

"There are three in here," Erica says. Not sure what she means, I glance over and see her with the paper bag wide open, examining its contents. She reaches in and pulls out a small pastry wrapped in waxy tissue, tugging at the paper to see what went wrong. "Did you order extra? Did they make a mistake? Jeremy, you should take this one back."

I shake my head and look at him, and I can't help it as a crooked smile breaks free. Typical Jeremy. His eyes meet mine as he reaches over to take it from her. "I thought Lauren might like one. Far as I know, you're still looking for work, right?"

I nod and take the pastry from him. I don't need

to see what it is. He knows my favorite—white chocolate scones with raspberry glaze. This shop is the only place in the city that makes them, and he used to bring them over for my marathon study sessions. He would knock on the door when he knew I had a major project due or test coming up, hand me the bag, grin, kiss me on the forehead, and leave without saying a word. The more I think about it, the more I have to wonder why I let him get away.

Then an image flashes in my mind, the vision of a beautiful face that will always haunt me. A face I thought I'd see forever, the one I wanted to wake up next to every morning for the rest of my life. The one that made me believe in soul mates.

Until it ended.

That's why I had to walk away. Jeremy is perfect in every possible way, from his steely blue eyes and boyish charm to his loving, thoughtful gestures and passionate kisses. But he's not perfect *for me*.

I think my eyes might be getting misty, so I hold

up the scone with a smile. I stand on tip toe to kiss him on the cheek and whisper, "Thank you, Jeremy. For everything. I never deserved you, so I really hope you find happiness with Erica. Give her a chance."

My lips brush his ear lobe. I want to offer one final kiss goodbye but I know I can't. It wouldn't be fair to Erica. I hear him sigh, as if he knows what I'm thinking and wants it, too. He puts an arm around me just briefly, but I back away. I can't look him in the eye again.

"You two crazy kids have fun tonight," I say, my voice too loud and full of false bravado. I throw on my game show hostess smile again. It feels forced, but at this point it's all I can manage. I watch them walk out, hand in hand, listening to the door jingle as they go.

DON JUAN GONE HORRIBLY WRONG

I plop down at my next assigned table, set down the scone, and stare at the card in my hand. Its edges are folding up, warping thanks to my sweaty palms and tendency to nervously crinkle it up in clenched fists when I'm trying to dodge another panic attack. How much more bizarre and stress inducing can this night possibly get? Yes, I needed to get off the couch and do something with myself, but it seems like my efforts should be met with something a little kinder than the universe's sick attempt at a practical joke.

I stop mid-thought. Whenever I ask the universe how much worse it can get, the universe brings it. I jinx myself every single time. It's like some cosmic force out there cracks its knuckles at me and says, "Challenge accepted." I focus on the card again and close my eyes, waiting.

The table shakes and tips in my direction, and I hear the rustling of someone sitting down across from me. I look up, and then sit back to take in Guy #3. I really hope he's rocking the hipster look in the extreme on purpose, because this guy's buttoned up-to-there plaid shirt and gray sweater vest make the eyeball guy look pretty hot in comparison. This guy is wearing black horn-rimmed glasses without any lenses in them, and his untrimmed beard is sparse and thin. It's entirely possible we go to the same stylist because he has my hairdo minus the blonde.

"Oh, wait a minute!" His voice is rather high pitched with a nasal pinch to it. He stands and takes off a canvas messenger bag, tossing it over the back of his black wooden chair. As he does I can see he's pegged and rolled up his jeans, and he has on deck shoes *sans* socks. He's skinny, so all his clothes practically fall off of him.

He sits back down and leans forward. "Hi, I'm Lennon."

"Aw, you're named after my favorite Beatle. I'm Lauren."

"I am. So glad you got the reference! Some people have zero taste in music, you know?" He has a slight lisp, but it's not on my nerves. Yet. "It's so great to meet you. I've been watching you all night so I'm, like, stoked to meet you."

"I'm not sure if I should be flattered or take out a restraining order."

He throws his head back and laughs like it's the funniest thing he's ever heard. I cock an eyebrow and lean back. Restraining order looks like it might be an actual possibility.

"O.M.G., that is seriously the funniest thing I've heard all night! You're amazing!"

"O.M.G.?" I raise my eyebrows. "Are you kidding me? We can speak in acronyms now?"

He laughs even harder, gripping his side like he's getting a cramp from running laps. My face falls and I close my eyes. Why does it feel like I'm getting punked by life right now? "Lauren, you are seriously too much."

"Okay, then...tell me, Lennon, what do you do?"

"I'm 27 and I'm getting ready to start grad school, after taking time off to explore my options. I think it's criminal that we should have to choose one career path and only study that one thing, you know? Life is just too beautiful to have to limit ourselves by the boxes we check on an aptitude test."

Translation: I'm a perennial student living in my parents' basement, spending more time in virtual reality than anywhere else.

I decide to play nice, though, thinking the universe might really go nutballs on me if I try to mess with him like I did the last guy.

"I hear you," I say, trying to be polite. "What interests you right now?"

"Seriously? Everything. I want to study it all.

My undergrad was in women's studies and I started a master's program in Russian literature, but I didn't want to pigeon hole myself so young. I took a few classes in human factors, but that didn't feel like the right fit either. I'm thinking I might try a class in social psychology this fall."

I nod in approval. "We have a great program here. I just graduated with my master's."

He leans forward eagerly. "Really? That's so interesting. Brains and beauty—I love it! What do you plan to do with it? Are you considering a PhD?"

I shake my head and laugh. "No, I think I'm sick of school. I'd like to work with at-risk kids in shelters, maybe counsel foster kids. They're the ones we tend to forget as a society."

"So true, so true," he murmurs. His head is tipped down but his eyes stay fixed on me, and he's really starting to creep me out with that 'come hither' expression he's wearing. It works on the cover of a romance novel, maybe, if you're a shirtless Viking, but in a scrawny dude with tight plaid buttoned up to the neck? Not so much. I look away and take a deep breath, trying not to shudder as something uncomfortable races down my spine.

I really have nothing to say to him anymore. I glance at the pastry Jeremy gave me, and I look down as a smile plays across my lips when I remember his kindness. I reach out and play with the tissue paper absent mindedly, hoping Lennon will take up the rest of the time because I got nothing. It occurs to me that he might mistake my smile for encouragement. My brow furrows and I frown, but when my eyes meet his I know it's too late. The wrong signal has been sent.

I'm guessing this won't end well, considering my track record so far this evening.

"What is this?" he asks, reaching forward to take my hand. He's a little awkward and smashes the scone into the paper, smearing white chocolate and raspberry glaze on both our hands as he does. I sigh and look sadly at my squashed scone. I think it's symbolic of my life at the moment. I reach for a napkin to wipe up the mess.

"Lennon, I need to run to the ladies room to wash my hands. I'll be right—"

"No, Lauren, don't leave! I can take care of it." He reaches into the man purse and pulls out a package of wet wipes. I have just a moment to ask myself if that's a man bag or a diaper bag before he grasps my hand. He caresses it lightly while trying to wipe up the mess, but instead of the romantic moment I guess he's trying to create, he accidentally smears the raspberry sauce even more all over the back of my hand.

"Sorry!"

I get up and clutch my purse before he can grab my hand again. "Really. It'll just take me a minute."

"I'm so sorry. I'll get you another while you're in the ladies room."

"Not necessary."

"I insist!"

I walk back to the bathroom as quickly as I can. I pray for a long line to delay me, but there's just one girl who looks as frazzled as I feel standing in front of one the sinks. She's average height with curly brown hair and pretty brown eyes, and wears a great pair of skinny jeans, a blazer with rolled up sleeves, and some seriously wicked high-heeled boots. She's slowly and very thoroughly working bubbles over her hands, bangle bracelets jangling with every move she makes. The soap makes a sickening, squishing noise as it runs through her fingers. She stands there, like she's mesmerized, staring blankly as I squirt some foam soap into my own hands and mirror her gestures.

After a moment she looks over. She takes a deep breath and starts to rinse off her hands. "So...what brings you in here?"

"A hipster guy with a pre-pubescent beard, lisp, a man purse, and attitude glasses thinking he's the next Don Juan DeMarco. He tried to hold my hand, and my scone got squashed, taking one for the team. I'm just washing off the mess. You?"

She laughs. "A guy with the nastiest looking eyeball I have ever seen spilled some coffee on the table. I didn't get any on me but I didn't tell him that. I just wanted an excuse to hide for a bit."

"Oh, yes. Kevin." I laugh. "He was my first date tonight. He's harmless, I think...just completely whackadoodle. Are you a his new friend, too? Has he hinted that you just might be *the one* yet?"

She rolled her eyes. "Uh, yeah. My sister dragged me here and is finding seriously fab guys while I keep getting the weirdos."

"Preach it, sister. Good luck." I grab a few paper towels to dry my hands. Crumpling them into a ball, I toss the wad into the trash can and back up toward the door. "You going out there again?"

She shakes her head with pursed lips. "No. My hands are *way* too dirty for that. Good luck with your...uh..."

"My little Casanova wannabe," I finish as I bump the bathroom door open with my booty and gird my loins for the rest of the round. I don't actually know what that means, but it sounds like suffering is involved in what happens next, and that sounds right to me. Maybe I can ponder the origins of such an odd saying to pass the time.

When I return, Lennon has replaced my scone

and placed a cup at my seat. I grasp the steaming mug covered with whipped cream and take a sip, surprised when I taste steamed milk with a hint of nutmeg and cinnamon. "This is thoughtful. Thank you."

"I thought you might like this," he murmurs, looking deep into my eyes. Oh, dear...I think I should have stayed in the bathroom. He looks awfully amorous. I sit down and lean forward, with my elbows on the table to grasp my mug with both hands. I set it down and realize my mistake a split second later. He lunges forward, grabs my hand, and pulls me close as he leans in. Using his free hand, he breaks off the corner of the pastry and bites into it, making moaning noises as he does.

May I please gouge out my eardrums? I close my eyes, pinch my lips, and turn away. I can't even watch it and my ears want to bleed at the bizarre noises he's making to demonstrate how delicious it is.

"This is so amazing," he whispers gruffly. "You need to try this."

I shake my head vigorously. "No, really, I'm good. You enjoy it." I open my eyes to look at him, trying to convey how much I really don't need to share the scone. Tactical error. He lifts another bite of scone to my lips and shoves it in while I'm protesting. I frown and try to swallow, and as I do he pulls his fingers back and licks them with that same disturbing moan of pleasure.

I yank my hand back and take my mug again, holding it close to my lips and blowing on it. If he tries that again he'll spill scalding liquid on me, and I hope he's smart enough to know spilling hot milk on his date won't earn him any points later. I pull my elbows close and hunch my shoulders, hoping my time is almost up.

"Was that scone everything you hoped it would be?" He raises his eyebrows and puckers his lips, throwing me his best attempt at bedroom eyes.

"I couldn't even begin to describe that," I say honestly. I close my eyes and shake my head in disgust. "Thanks again for the steamer, Lennon. I appreciate it, but—"

"Did you know cinnamon oil has been used for centuries in ancient mating rituals?" He leans forward, head down again, his eyes shooting what he probably thinks are love darts at me. "I took a class on it for my major. So fascinating! Cinnamon was used in some cultures as part of fertility rituals. The male would take just a drop of oil and dab it on his—"

The bell rings, drowning out what he whispers in my ear. I throw up in my mouth a little and swallow hard. He stands and moves forward to kiss my cheek. "I hope we'll see each other again soon, Lauren. You and I have some unfinished business."

My nostrils flare. I am so tempted to tell him off, but that won't do any good. Instead, I grab my purse and my little card, making sure he sees me mark 'no' next to his name before I stalk away. It's official—I can never eat cinnamon again. I pull my phone out of my purse and rattle off a quick text to Harlow: *You're dead to me.*

THE ONE

I'm close to tears. Why does pushing myself out of my comfort zone have to be so hard? It's physically painful. My chest hurts and my head pounds, and it's hard to breathe. I'm feeling close to where I was at the end of round one, with another panic attack knocking at the back door.

It's not worth it. Finding someone just isn't worth the effort and sacrifices we make to find each other. Why am I even here looking? I don't need someone just for the sake of being with someone....anyone! Dating is like dumpster diving—there may be something good somewhere, but you have to sift through a ridiculous amount of disgusting things to get there. The payback doesn't seem worth getting covered in figurative coffee grounds, half-eaten donuts, and banana peels.

I look at the card in my hand and look at my table number for Round 4. If the next one gives off anything like a creeper vibe, I'm out of here. I don't care if I spend the rest of my life living alone on my smelly sofa. I will find personal fulfillment in becoming one with the furniture.

A guy walks up to the table I'm watching and sits down. His back is to me, and I can't get a good look at his face. It's up by the front window and he's looking out at the street, away from me, while others in the shop work their way to their own tables to get started. They're blocking my view so I can't get a good read on him. From the back he looks a lot like Grant, and my heart does that crazy, irrational thud it always does when I think of him.

And then he turns around to scan the crowd. My heart starts beating so hard it feels like it's trying to pound its way out of my rib cage.

It *is* Grant.

As the eyeball guy would say, he was *the one*. I spent three years of my life believing that with all my soul. Grant and I were so alike, so perfectly complementary, that no one else would ever come close. Even great guys like Jeremy will never compare. When we were together, I believed in soul mates. I believed in forever.

I stare hard at the table number, staying hidden in the shadows at the back of the shop while he turns back around and waits. I take a closer look at my card just to make sure he's my next date. Yes, he's sitting there at my table, waiting patiently for me to show up.

He looks amazing. I haven't seen him in five years now, not since the night he took me to the emergency room, dropped me off, and walked away. As I think back to what I put him through those last few months we were together, I guess I can't blame him for not coming back.

His hair is shorter now, cut close to the back of his head, with some crazy sexy sideburns and a little lift on top. I loved running my fingers through those brown curls back in the day. My mind flashes to another time and I can feel those curls in my fingers, feel his soft lips against mine, feel our hearts beating in time with each other. He turns again to look around, those green eyes flashing. His impish grin is the same, although I see the start of a smile line on one side of his face, and little crinkles starting at the corners of his eyes. He's tan, wearing a pair of loose jeans and a burgundy dress shirt, collar open. He's never looked so good.

Seeing him soothes my panic, even though it also makes it practically impossible to breathe. He was always the balm my soul needed, especially right before my emotional implosion. I take a deep breath and emerge from the shadows. He looks out the window again, probably thinking he just got stood up now that everyone else has settled down. The dim buzz of hushed conversation fills the air as I reach for the chair and lean forward. My hands rest on the chair back as I look down.

"Grant Fierro, you're never going to believe

who your date is this round."

Surprise, confusion, and a little terror register on his face. He's speechless. I'm suddenly thankful I spotted him and had a moment to prepare myself to see him after so much time. He's completely blindsided. No matter how justified he was to drop me off and never look back, I'm not the one who walked out on us. I'm not the one who abandoned all the promises we made without anything close to a goodbye. I owe him nothing. He's the one who has explaining to do, and no time to really think what he might say when we saw each other.

It takes him a moment to collect his thoughts. I sit down before he has the chance to stand up and hug me in greeting, because I know his dad raised him to be a gentleman and that's his first move.

"Lauren Brooks, I can't believe it. It's been a really long time."

"No kidding." I glance casually at my watch. "Only five years or so. What have you been up to?"

Specifically, what happened after you dumped me at the hospital without telling me I just got dumped?

"You're the last person I expected to see here." He's at a loss for words, something that never happens.

"Thought I'd still be locked up in the wacky shack? I guess I can't blame you there. I was pretty crazy last time I saw you."

He shakes his head with a smile. "I forgot how direct you can be. It's great to see you. It's been a really long time."

"You already said that, but it's okay. I know I'm intimidating."

Grant's eyes shine at me, just like they used to, and I bite my lip. I expected this to be much more awkward. Why does he still have to be so incredibly handsome?

I lean forward, elbows on the table as I move closer. Despite what happened, he's always been one of my favorite people and I want to hear how he's doing, make sure life's been kind to him. He's one of the few in this world who deserves a happily ever after.

"Tell me what you've been up to for the last few years. Last time we saw each other, you were getting ready to graduate with a double major in political science and economics. You planned to reform all the corrupt politicians. Every last one of them." He leans back and laughs, his head tipped back, and I'm surprised at the sheer abandon of it. "Your grand ideas and fierce ambition were going to transform D.C. and make the world a better place. What are you doing back here?"

"I lasted a year on Capitol Hill," he admits ruefully. He runs his fingers through his hair and shakes his head as he leans back. He tilts his head thoughtfully to one side to look at me, giving me a sidelong glance. "I came back to law school and finished up a few weeks ago. When I'm not studying for the bar, I spend my time having coffee with psychos and miscreants here for a little Friday night adventure. Do I know how to party or what?"

"So you make this 5 in 5 thing a habit?" I ask with raised eyebrows. A man this hot and this spectacular should have no trouble finding dates.

Grant laughs. I miss that laugh. "No. This is actually my first time."

"Let me guess," I say. "Your roommate dragged you here under threat of death because you spend way too much time studying and not enough time doing the mating dance."

"You haven't changed one bit, Lauren."

I tilt my head and give him a sidelong look. "Considering the last time I saw you, I was being strapped to a gurney and drugged into oblivion, I hope I've changed just a little." My words make him uncomfortable, but he knows me well enough to know I'm honest. Sure, I live in denial a good portion of the time, but I have always believed in full frontal honesty with others.

"Lauren, I..."

I hold up a hand to stop him. "It's okay, Grant, really. You saved me. I was death spiraling and you were the one who helped me when I needed it most. Thank you." It must be emotional resolution night, with Jeremy and now Grant, but it feels liberating to tell him how much it means to me that he made the hard choice to have me committed. "I'm in a much better place now, you know? I'm finally healthy. You got me the help I needed. No one knew how sick I was until I snapped."

"You look different," he says, changing the subject and appraising me from across the table. "This is the Lauren I remember." He reaches into his wallet and pulls out a bent and faded picture, black and white, from those cheap photo booths at the mall. We were best friends all through high school, and this was one of those blissful days where we had cash in our pockets and time to kill.

In this picture, he's kissing my cheek and my eyes are wide open, mouth forming a perfect circle as I pretend to be surprised. Long, frizzy, ash blonde hair spills down my shoulders and out of the picture, and my hazel eyes are coated in more black eye liner than anyone should wear in a month. His trademark backwards ball cap is pushed up on his head as he kisses me, and his eyes turn sideways, gleaming for the camera, while his brows slant playfully up.

"It's the new Lauren," I say with a shrug as I gingerly take the photo from him and stare. This was just before high school graduation, right around the time we decided we were much more than friends.

"You look fantastic," he says.

"Well, I'm healthy. I really am. Much healthier than I was when we...well, I had to make up some classes after my emotional train wreck, but I got a degree in psychology and just finished up a master's in counseling."

He looks taken aback. "Wow, I didn't see that one coming!"

I hand back the image, that carefree moment in time frozen on film. His hand brushes mine for just a moment as he takes it back, and a jolt, hot like wildfire, rushes through my veins. "After you dropped me like a hot—" I begin, but he cuts me off.

"I did what I thought I had to do, Lauren. You were sick." I can tell I've made his guard shoot up. He pulls away, looking agitated, and I don't want him on the defensive.

I laugh, not quite sure what else to do. "I know! Seriously, I can't thank you enough for what you did. I spent a few weeks in the psych ward there, and then moved to residential rehab for some more intensive treatment. I lived there about a year. But the staff was so amazing...they inspired me to help others. I'm still looking for work, but I'd like to help troubled teens, especially homeless girls and foster kids, help them before they have a psychotic break like I did. Not every girl has an amazing boyfriend like you to rescue them. Well...when I had you." I look down. "So many of them just have pimps, you know? If I can save just one girl from a life on the streets, it'll be worth it to me."

"I lied," he says quietly, looking away and shaking his head. "You've changed quite a bit."

"I hope so. Crazy girls are only fun at parties."

Silence falls between us and the air feels heavy with the weight of what could have been. I guess sometimes things really are better left unsaid. It's comfortable and awful all at the same time, being with him again. After so much time apart, I shouldn't expect that feeling of belonging to stay. Tears start to well up in my eyes and I'm mad at myself for letting them form. He'll think I'm still psycho girl if I let them fall.

He slides another picture across the table to me. I snigger and wipe my eyes, hoping he thinks it's because I'm laughing at the memory. It's our prom picture—we went together as a joke. He's wearing his grandpa's vintage 1970's polyester tux, in the single most wretched shade of powder blue ever invented, with ruffles down the front of the revolting long-collared shirt. I stole his black and white checkered fedora for the picture, and it's perched at a jaunty angle on my head.

I have on a ridiculous black dress with a skirt cut so high I wouldn't need to change into a gown at the gynecologist, but the strapless, sequined gown is covered with a long-sleeved, lacy black bolero hanging off my too-thin frame. I'm holding the ends of it in my hands as he holds mine in the picture. I had already started cutting myself by then and stupidly thought wearing long sleeves would keep people from seeing the angry red slashes all over my arms. I hadn't started putting matches out on the backs of my hands when this pic was taken, but it wasn't long after. I told everyone I was allergic to bug bites when they called me on it. Everyone bought my lies except Grant. He never said anything, but I knew he could see through my words.

"Look at us, grinning like dorks," I say, passing it back.

"We had fun, right? I can't believe we didn't end up in jail for some of our stunts."

"That's where we belonged, really," I agree. "Whose bright idea was it to go shopping cart bombing, anyway?"

"I do believe that was Oliver's brilliant scheme." He sighs with a grin, the one I remember so well. The one that made me fall hard for him. "Vandalism at its finest."

"Oliver," I sigh. "I miss that little troll. Whatever happened to him?"

"He's here tonight," Grant says, turning in his chair to point at a table on the side, next to the brick wall near the ladies room.

"Seriously?" I squeal, spinning around to look for him. "I have to talk to him!"

"We're roomies. Have been since I moved back for law school."

"Oh man," I say as I catch Oliver's eye and wink at him. He gives me a confused look and keeps chatting up his date. I realize he probably has no idea who I am, since I have short dyed hair, a nose stud, and something resembling a chest now. "We had good times, didn't we?"

"We did."

It gets quiet again, and we spend a few moments saying nothing before the bell rings and we're done. My heart breaks a little as Grant stands up and offers me a quick, back-patting hug before hurrying to the men's room. Despite everything left unsaid, he still feels right. Good. Comfortable. Seeing him feels like putting on a pair of my favorite jeans. It's always been the perfect fit for me.

I'm flustered and can't think straight as I watch him vanish into the restroom. I reach for my purse but knock it to the ground instead. Change rolls everywhere and I have to crawl on the floor to collect it while people are walking around or milling about at tables. I'm gonna get trampled if I don't hurry...plus, I just want to evaporate.

I gather everything in one big sweep of the arm and shove it all back into my bag before I hurry away. I can't do the last round, no matter what I told myself. I'm gonna tap out and let the universe have this one. Ten crazy guys would wreak less emotional havoc on me than one moment looking into the vivid green of Grant Fierro's gorgeous eyes.

WORTH THE RISK

I reach into my purse for my phone as I head toward the front door. I pick it up to see a text from Harlow glowing on the screen. *I'm sorry you're having a bad time, but this guy so far is worth every bad date I've ever had. *sigh* I'm a little gone on this one!*

I can't help but smile. She's dated way too many guys who were only using her for her power and connections. I pull up my on-screen keyboard and text back. *I'm thrilled for you, but you might want to sleep with the lights on tonight. You've been warned.*

There's a sleek silver trash can just by the exit. I stop to drop in the feedback card I was given when I walked in and registered for the 5 in 5 fiasco. I don't care who wants my number. I don't want anyone to call me. I don't even want the free coffee. I just want to go home and shower this night off.

"Excuse me, please. Pardon!"

I turn around to see the eyeball guy heading out, holding hands with someone. I stop to take her in. If I saw this woman on the street, in her sensible shoes, denim jumper, cardigan, and out of control red curls pulled back into a low, long braid down her back, I'd probably look at her just long enough to realize someone else was there. I'd judge her on her appearance, call her mousy, feel a moment of pity for her inferior DNA, and then forget she exists as I go about my day. When I see her and the eyeball guy together, though, she looks completely radiant.

I stare at them as they move past me, and I cock my head to the side as I try to figure out how that happened. They're both glowing as they inch toward the door, trying to sneak out as people get settled for the last round,. I can't help but notice how attractive they suddenly both seem. Maybe attractive isn't the right word, not in the magazine cover sense of the word...but the happiness they exude makes me not care how they look at all. I'm sort of stunned by this revelation.

"Kevin!" I call as they reach the front door.

He turns around, suddenly looking embarrassed when he recognizes me. "Oh, hello, Lauren." His companion looks at him expectantly. "Tessa, I'd like you to meet Lauren. She was my first date tonight."

I extend a hand and shake hers. "It looks like you two are trying to sneak out of the last round."

"Well...uh..." He looks at the card still in his other hand, where I see my number along with three others with a dark X next to the yes box our names. He tosses his into the trash, too. "Tessa, why don't you wait for me at the bus stop? I'd like to say goodbye to my friend Lauren."

She nods and ducks out, and I have to wonder

how he got her to speak enough to feel like they made a connection.

"Kevin, I have a random question. Well, maybe not totally random. I mean, I guess it goes with what we talked about earlier." I really should come with my own teleprompter. Nothing is coming out right.

He holds up a hand. He's dangerously close to shushing me with that devil finger of his again, but I step back just in time. "Lauren, I'll always cherish our time together. You're the nicest person I met here tonight, other than Tessa, and you know you can never have too many friends!"

My eyes open wide in shock. Does he think I'm jealous? "Oh, no, no! I just wanted to—"

Kevin offers me a sad little shake of his head. "I think you and I will always be just friends. But when I met Tessa, something about her just felt right. I think she just might be—"

"The one?" I finish. I have to smile at his eager and happy grin. "That's what I wanted to ask you about, Kevin." I look down. "I used to believe in the one, but now I don't know. How do you...know? And what if you think you have it and you throw it away? What then?"

I'm asking the weirdest person I've ever met if he knows the mysteries of the universe. What's wrong with me?

He takes my question seriously, however, if his drawn eyebrows and bemused expression mean anything. "Here's my opinion, and you can take it or leave it. I think just about anyone can be *the one*, but the one for what? That's the question, isn't it? Maybe Tessa is *the one*, or the girl to help me prepare for *the one*, and maybe she's just the one for coffee and conversation tonight. I think I'll know more later. You can't find anyone if you don't try. It's always worth it to try, don't you think?"

"So you're saying it's always worth the risk?"

"I am."

"And you're not worried about getting hurt?"

He snorts at my question, even though his gentle eyes show no malice. "Sure, I am. Aren't we all? But a wise person once said that the greatest blessings come from taking the biggest risks. 'The person who risks nothing, does nothing, is nothing and becomes nothing.'"

I raise my eyebrows in surprise, and one corner of my mouth turns up in an appreciative smile. I used that very quote in one of my papers. "Leo Buscaglia," I say.

Kevin nods. "He also said something like if you close your arms to love, you'll be left only holding yourself. And what kind of life would that be?" He glances out the window and grins at the woman waving anxiously at him as a bus appears around the corner and pulls toward the stop. "Most people don't get me, but my arms are wide open. Open your arms, Lauren. You might be surprised."

I watch him hurry toward her and place his hand protectively on the small of her back as she climbs up the steps. He follows her onto the idling bus. The door jerks shut behind them and the bus lurches forward before it disappears around the corner in a puff of black exhaust. Kevin could be the poster boy for that old saying 'there's a fine line between genius and madness,' but his words resonate with me in an unexpected way.

He's right.

I've been spending too much time since it all happened with my arms folded tight to my chest. I've closed myself off to life. I thought I was living again, but now it's starting to feel like I'm only taking up space. I don't want to be a waste of oxygen anymore. I think I'm finally ready for things to change.

I guess the only question is whether or not I have the courage to do anything about it.

JULI CALDWELL

THE LITTLE GUY

As I reach the front door and again start to push it open, the phone vibrates in my hand. I pause long enough to check out the message, nothing more than an LOL from Harlow in reply to my earlier text. I shove it back into its pocket deep inside my abyss of a handbag when I hear a sound that can only be described as bizarre...but familiar.

I freeze when I hear a manly voice in falsetto screeching, "Eee-er! Eee-er! Eee-er!" from somewhere near the back of the coffee shop, and I have no choice but to burst out laughing. I turn around, shaking because I'm laughing so hard, and I see my old friend Oliver standing on a chair. His hands are cupped around his mouth and he's shrieking out the call we used in high school to find each other in the overcrowded halls.

"Eeeeee-errrrr!" I squawk back. I could never do it as well as he could, so I sound ridiculous. The people around us are looking confused and a little annoyed at the hideous sound, but at the moment I care as much about their opinions as I would've back in high school.

Oliver jumps off the chair and shoves his way through the crowd to give me his famous tackling bear hug. He's super short, just 5', making me feel like a giant at my completely average 5'5". He grabs me around the waist and rocks me back and forth.

"You're such a perv, Oliver. I know you're just hugging me to get closer to the ladies."

"Psh," he scoffs. "You don't have any ladies." He stands back to look me over, and then laughs and hugs me again. "Oh, look! The boob fairy finally waved her magic wand over you.

Congratulations!" I slap him and he laughs, hugging me again. "Laur, you look amazing! What are you doing here?"

"Right now I'm trying to escape."

"Aw, don't leave now! The fun's just starting! I've convinced four women that I'm a circus midget and asked them to come on the road with me as the bearded lady. I promised them fame, adventure, and a litter of small, hairy children. Oddly, I have no takers."

I burst out laughing again. "Oh, man! How did we ever lose touch?"

"Don't leave!" he begs, grabbing my hand and pulling me away from the door.

"I think I'm done," I say with a shrug. "You should've caught me two rounds ago, when I was still making an effort to be in the moment at this psychotic meat market."

He's pretty insistent, however, and he drags me to the table where I sat just moments before with Grant. "No, you can't leave until we catch up and I have your digits. I'm not losing my *tout-puissante* again. Ever."

"Well, *secundum ver-bumtum* to you," I say, finishing the line. My ribs ache and I have a stitch in my side from laughing so hard. I forgot how amazing it feels to laugh so freely, to laugh and mean it. He's quoting old choir songs, something we did to pretend we spoke another language as we walked from class to class. We thought we were über cool and different, but I suddenly realize we were more ridiculous than I ever imagined. "We were idiots, you know that?"

He wags his eyebrows at me. "Still are, I hope. Nothing like a little nonconformity to keep it real."

"How are you?" I ask.

Oliver pulls a face and smacks his forehead. "How am I? Cheese and rice, woman, that's the kind of question you ask people you hardly know at a twenty year reunion," he says. "Try again."

I raise my eyebrows and do my best. "Hey, wazzup?"

He nods approvingly. "That's what I'm talking about! So, you won't believe this, but...I'm the choir teacher now."

My jaw drops. "At Lincoln High? No way! That's so funny...you always swore once we got out of there you'd never, ever step foot in that cement death-trap of a school again. And now you're a teacher? What parallel universe am I trapped in? You've become the arch nemesis! You're the new Miss Benson!"

"I have better cleavage, though."

I snicker. I missed this guy.

He glances back toward the men's room. I follow his gaze and realize Grant is now the one hiding in the bathroom, which pleases me in a very weird way. "So, Grant says you're a shrink now. We might have openings for a school counselor if you're interested, if you're looking for work."

"I don't have the right endorsement, but thanks. I'm thinking I'm a halfway house kind of girl, anyway."

"Gotta save those lost souls since you used to be one yourself?"

I look down. "Was it that obvious? I thought I

hid it so well."

"You did. Looking back, it should have been apparent. I guess we all have 20/20 hindsight."

I sit back and fold my arms, looking into the distance as my eyes glaze over and my vision blurs just a bit. It's my defense mechanism, my way of detaching from whatever scares me. Zone out and ignore reality. I have to shake my head to pull out of it. "Go ahead and ask, Ollsie. I have no more secrets."

He leans forward earnestly. He's all about laying it on the table, like I am, so I prepare myself mentally for the onslaught. I can't help but smile at him, though. We've known each other since kindergarten and we always stood up for each other. He had my back; I had his. He got teased for being short, and I got mocked for being too skinny. All legs, no boobs. We were each other's fiercest defenders.

When Grant joined us in middle school a few years later, we had another misfit to defend. We were all so gawky and awkward, but I'm looking at

Oliver and thinking I don't care how short he is. He's hot. He has thick blond hair, blue eyes so light they're almost white, the pupils ringed with a circle of black, and a ruddy complexion. He has eyelashes girls like me would kill for, and a perfect smile with gleaming teeth. He's stocky and muscular without an ounce of fat on him. I smile at him. "How did an annoying little troll like you get to be so devastatingly handsome?" I ask.

"I work out under my troll bridge," he says, those eyes cutting through me. "Now talk. Here's what I know: I'm away at school, everything seems fine, all is cool, and suddenly Grant calls me out of the blue to say your sister was killed, you tried to commit suicide, and he just left you in the emergency room and thought they would be admitting you to the psych ward for awhile."

I pinch my lips together and take a deep breath. "Sounds about right," I say with a shake of the head, wrenching my neck too far and too fast but I mask it as a hair flip, pretending I don't want my hair to fall in my eyes. Anything to look away.

He watches me expectantly. When I don't elaborate, his cheeks flush. "I need the dirt, Laur."

I've hashed this all out with my therapist, and I've accepted it. I'm not sure who the old Lauren was, because she was so sick that she really had no way to know herself. The person I am, the woman sitting in front of an old friend, is sort of a creation. She didn't exist last time this this guy saw her. Tears pool in my eyes. They want to fall, and it will feel so good to let them go, but I grit my teeth and bite them back. Talking to my therapist seems easy compared with facing the truth of who I was and what happened with people I knew best.

I look down and swallow hard. I shake my head, mad at myself. Mad that I have to tell anyone else. Mad that I'm still mad at myself. Mad that I've accepted what happened and made a life for myself without my sister.

"Coral was killed in a motorcycle accident. She went to this party and met a guy who was way too old and driving way too fast on his bullet bike, showing off for the girls. He decides my sweet and innocent baby sister is worthy of his affection, and he talks her into going for a little ride around the neighborhood. She was only fifteen, Oliver. Her life hadn't even started. She meets this bonehead loser who's hot-dogging to impress the girls...and they crash. The police figured he was going around 130 when he hit the curve and lost control. She was dead and it was all my fault."

He shakes his head vigorously. "No way, Lauren. I mean, do you hear yourself? It's not your fault some idiot wrecked his bike."

I bite my lip as the tears well in my eyes again. I refuse to let them fall. "No, it really is," I whisper. "My parents told her she couldn't go to that party. I had her come to my dorm for a slumber party instead...so she could go. I snuck her out while telling my parents we were just having a sister bonding night. Pajamas and popcorn. Nothing could be more innocent, right?" I sniffle. "I drove her there and told her to have fun, get crazy, and I'd come back around three o'clock to get her. My parents had to go identify her body around three instead." I snuffle again and grab my purse, hoping I can find a tissue somewhere in there. I'm looking just for the sake of doing something other than talking.

"Oh, man," he says. He sits back and shoves both his hands through his hair with a heavy sigh. He looks up at the ceiling as he processes what I just said. "And...what about you?"

I laugh as I sniffle a bit. My eyes feel bloodshot and I'm looking up to avoid making eye contact. I finally locate a tissue and wipe my runny nose. I sniffle again. "Turns out I was quite the head case already. I didn't know it, of course, but her death made me snap. I had a psychotic break. The night of Coral's funeral....I spent that night under the dining room table at Grant's apartment, screaming that I was surrounded. It felt so real, those images so vivid. I swear I was surrounded by faceless creatures in red, hooded robes, and Coral was telling me to come and join her. Grant was fantastic. He was so sweet, talked to me, tried to get me out. I think he finally went to call the cops for help when I ran from under the table and locked myself in the bathroom, where I promptly swallowed every single pill I could find."

Oliver's eyes are wide in disbelief. "I don't know what to say."

"You don't have to say anything, " I tell him simply. "It happened. It's over. This is my reality now. Mental illness is like cancer in some ways. When you're as messed up as I am, you have good days and bad days, even on the meds. When I'm good, it's like being in remission. My roommate Harlow knows what's up and she lets me know if she sees anything suspicious where I need to get some extra help to get back on track."

"So...what do you have?"

I grin, but it's an empty one. It's more like laughing politely at a joke that's not close to being funny. "What don't I have? Bipolar two and a little self-mutilation, with a side of anxiety disorder. Your eyes are ready to pop out of your head, man. Blink, will you?"

"I can't believe none of us ever saw any signs

that something was wrong. I mean, we all thought you were crazy, but it was good, fun crazy, like you were a party of one that never stopped."

I raise my eyebrows. "One of the hallmark signs of bipolar two."

"I had no idea. None of us did."

"I tried to hide it from Grant. I made sure to hide all the crazy, even from him, and we'd been together for years. I don't blame him at all for walking away and not looking back."

"You're wrong," Oliver says. He shakes his head at me, blond locks tossed back as he does. "He didn't just walk away. Grant never would have walked away from you."

UNHIDDEN TRUTH

I tip my head to the side and look at him, confused. "What do you mean?"

Oliver leans forward again and looks at me thoughtfully. "How much do you remember about those first few days at the hospital?"

"Not much," I admit with a shake of the head. "I was really out of it because of the OD and all the drugs they put me on. I remember more once I got on the psych floor."

"Grant was there for the first few days," Oliver tells me. "He called and texted me updates all the time. When you were starting to come out of it, he said your parents pulled him aside and asked that he step out of the picture so you could focus on getting well. He said things had been rough between you two for a while and he agreed it would be best if he didn't see you. It wrecked him, Laur. He wanted to be there with you every day, but he figured you'd look for him when you got out of residential rehab."

I never did.

I was so angry and hurt that I never heard a single word from him that I didn't even bother. Pride is kind of a vicious creature, and it's what kept me from looking. I never bothered to ask where he was or why he never came, maybe because I thought if I meant something to him, he would put the effort into seeing me. When he didn't, I adopted a good riddance attitude even though my heart ached to see him, to find out why, even though I figured I already knew.

I was horrible to him the last few months we were together. I know now it's because I was sick and not thinking clearly, but how could he know that? I'd gone from best friend and girlfriend to psycho beast in a short amount of time, and I didn't think I deserved another chance. I could think of twenty reasons for him not to want me anymore but not a single reason why he might.

My brow knots in concentration as I think back to the vague memories I have of the first few days of my recovery. I don't recall much from my drug-induced haze, but I dreamed of him every day. I dreamed he was holding my hand, stroking my fingers gently while he whispered that I would get through this and everything would be okay. He whispered plans of a future, one with both of us. Those hushed promises filled my heart with hope, and then shattered it when they never happened.

"I dreamed of him...or maybe what I thought were dreams actually happened. I don't know." I look Oliver square in the eyes and my head starts to throb from the effort of holding in the tears. "The last thing I dreamed before I went to the psych ward is...him. Us."

I'm lying in my bed, hospital gown haphazardly snapped up and the ties loose around my neck.

Several IV tubes shoot from my arm, snake around the bed, and spill off the edge before arching back up to connect with the bag of whatever pharmaceutical cocktail they're pumping into me. Everything around me is misty and dark, but I can feel someone's presence. I sense Axe body wash and coordinating cologne. If I could smile, I would, if only to let Grant know he's the world's least secret agent and I can tell he's there. I smell his trademark man-scent from a mile off.

The chair legs scrape against the linoleum floor with the creak of old wood as the aroma comes closer. Someone sits down beside me. Suddenly he's in my narrow field of vision, and all I see is his dark head of hair as he leans forward to kiss my hand, and tears drop onto my limp and exposed palm. They're warm but they chill my hand as they run off. I'm trying so hard to move, to touch him, to tell him to stop being a dork and get us a pizza so we can forget this ever happened.

"I'm sorry, Laur. I'm so sorry."

Quit being a tool and stop crying!

I want to say it, but the words won't come. I'm not dead...am I? I can't get any words out. My voice won't work. I can't say anything and it's annoying me. In the blur I can make out a fuzzy square of light that might be a window, but beyond that I see nothing. The rest is dark, but it doesn't matter. I don't want to see anything, and I'm happy not to feel anything. The drugs make me not feel the agony that envelopes me whenever I think of my sister. I can't breathe without shots of guilty pain stabbing my lungs. All I want is to tell Grant I'm okay and to stop crying because that makes me want to cry. And I hate crying.

"*This is for the best,*" *he's saying. I wish I could stroke his hair, and pull him into my arms. He must've read my mind because the bed creaks and lurches, and he's suddenly beside me, curled up next to me as I lie there like a corpse. He drapes his arm carefully over tubes and wires to stroke my cheek.*

What's for the best?

"*You need this time to get better. I know you—*

you'll understand why someday. It's not like I want to walk away. I'm not. I'll never walk away from you, or from us. When you need me, I'm here, even if you decide I'm the worst mistake you ever made. If you marry someone else, if you end up in jail, if you need me to hide a body, I'm there. Always. We have history, and I will always love you. If you come out of this and just want to be friends, that's cool. You, me, and Oliver will still be the three amigos. I..." He sighs heavily. *"You need to focus on getting better, work on becoming whole without being someone's girlfriend. You need to figure out who Lauren is and make her better so we can be together again."*

He snorts a little bit, and then sniffles as he pulls me closer. "That's what your mom said, anyway, and she's probably right. You know I never had one, but she's pretty cool so I think with her and your dad by your side, you'll pull through this. They're having a rough time right now, too...first Coral, and now you, so go easy on 'em. You're all they have left. I know how pissy you can get when you want something, but just let it go and focus on getting healthy again."

He shifts beside me and I feel his fingers caressing my face before he leans in and gently kisses my forehead. "Bye, Laur. Get better and I'll see you soon." The indent on the bed lifts as the warmth and weight next to me vanish, and the comforting smell of him is gone.

"I remember," I murmur as a rogue tear breaks free.

"He was there."

"Yeah...he was. I remember now," I repeat, nodding in agreement.

"So what now?" Oliver asks. He glances again toward the men's room but I can't bring myself to look that way. I'm afraid if I see Grant, my resolve will break and I'll go running to him. I'll beg forgiveness. I'll look like an idiot as I apologize and profess my undying love. He'll probably get a restraining order. He will thank his lucky stars I showed my crazy when I did so he could make a clean getaway. Five years have passed. I can't erase that time or make right everything I did wrong, even if that time didn't come close to erasing how I feel about him.

"What now?" I echo. I close my eyes for the briefest moment with a sad shake of my head. "Now I go home, Oliver. I give you my number and we can hang out. You make beautiful music with your choir students. Grant passes the bar and goes on to be the most amazing lawyer in the history of lawyers. I look for work and hopefully make a difference to someone in this awful world." I grab my purse and stand up. The bell rang a while ago, so the place has cleared out, although people still mill around between tables and talk quietly in shadowed corners. "Life goes on, Oliver. That's what happens now."

BEGIN AGAIN

I'm back in my place on the couch, with my denim jacket dangling off its arm. The cute white sundress is now lying in a crumpled heap on my bedroom floor, and my shoes are scattered between the kitchen and sofa. I do have on clean yoga pants with baggy tee shirt fresh from my drawer, something I hope Harlow's hypersensitive nose will appreciate.

The TV is off. My thoughts are racing as I stare at the popcorn ceiling, my eyes glazing over and blurring as I think. The little specks of glitter in the ceiling look like distant stars in my distorted vision, and I'm trying to focus only on that.

The door opens and slams shut. I hear the dead bolt slide shut and the chain rattle as Harlow locks up for the night. I reach for my phone to check the time, and hop up to greet her.

"So, how was your night with the engineer?" I ask as I walk into the hall. She's leaning against the door with a dreamy look on her face, eyes sparkling as she looks up.

She drops her purse on our little entry table and puts her hands on her head. "Lauren, I want to giggle and scream like a little girl. I don't even know what to think. I...I'm just gone on this guy."

"Harlow has a boyfriend, Harlow has a boyfriend," I chant in an obnoxious, sing-songy sort of way.

Harlow looks up and just laughs. "I think I might. It was so nice to be with a guy who wasn't playing games."

"And when are you seeing him again?"

She looks at me nervously, like I might judge her. "Tomorrow?"

"Wow. Good for you!" I say sincerely. I'm a little surprised she's moving this fast. She's always master of the calculated and thoughtful move, which is why she's so great at what she does at work. She'll probably own the place in five years. Who am I to judge her on the nerdy engineer boy? If she finds true love, or thinks it's something close to that, she needs to hold on tight and fight to hang onto it. I lost the best thing in my life because I didn't believe we were worth fighting for. As the eyeball guy would say, keep those arms open. Embrace the possibilities.

I head back to my daydreaming spot on the couch and pat the cushion next to mine, inviting her to join me. "I've seen way too many guys use you to get ahead or have a trophy on his arm. You shouldn't be paraded around for your looks or used for networking. You deserve a great guy. I'm glad we went tonight, if only so you could meet Pete."

Harlow pulls a face. She kicks off her stilettos and slides across the wooden floor to flop down on the couch. "When I got the text that said I was dead to you, I thought maybe you weren't so glad you went. What happened?"

I laugh. I hop up to grab a half-eaten pint of Ben and Jerry's from the freezer along with a couple of spoons, and then rejoin her by plopping down next to her. She takes a spoon from me as I pull off the lid, which I toss on the coffee table. We put our feet up and dig in. "I had a few epiphanies tonight."

"Really?" Harlow examines the spoon before loading it up and taking a bite. "How so? What do you mean?"

I stop and take a deep breath. I wish I could say I knew exactly when a switch flipped on in my head. I spent so much of my time tonight just trying to work through the emotions staging a steel cage death match in my head that I never noticed, I guess. I walked home alone under the orange glow of the street lamps, and my head cleared itself under stars not visible through city lights and fireflies dancing around me as I walked. Maybe seeing Grant was the last little bit of closure I needed to move on completely. He still takes my breath away.

I know now that I will always love him. This pain in my heart, the palpable twinge, the longing ache, hopefully will dim as time goes by. As lovers come and go. As memories fade a little bit every day.

"I saw him tonight."

"Him?" She raises her eyebrows at me and licks the back of her spoon before scraping the inside of the carton for another bite. "As in, *him* him?"

I nod and load my spoon again too. "The one I never talk about. Grant."

"He was there? Like he was doing the 5 in 5 thing, too?" She sits upright and turns to face me, a look of incredulity on her face. "Was he one of your dates?"

"Yup. Round four."

She buries her face in her hands while trying to keep the spoon out of her hair. "Lauren, I am so sorry! This is all my fault!"

I laugh. "Come on, Harlow. Think about it. How could you possibly have known that the guy I never told you about, whose existence you didn't know of until about ten seconds ago, would be at a dating event you dragged me to? You have nothing to be sorry for. And like I said," I tell her as I lean further to rest my head against the back of the couch, "It's all good. I had epiphanies and stuff."

She leans back with me. "Epiphanies and stuff," she repeats, sounding dubious. "So tell me, then, what epiphanies can a girl have while speed dating with socially awkward freak shows and long lost boyfriends?"

"I have to live the best life I can to honor my sister. I keep her alive through me."

Harlow shakes her head. "This is what you get from socially awkward freaks? Impressive! I should take you every week so we can find solutions to world hunger and a cure for cancer."

I laugh. "Not really, no, although the eyeball guy has a lot more to him than I ever would've imagined. He's living proof of why it's never a good idea to judge a book by its cover. Most people would burn that book after the first page." I scrape my spoon around the outside of the ice cream lump we've created in the middle of the carton, wanting to get the soft, melty goods for myself.

"Quit taking the best part," she protests, trying to grab the carton from me.

I let her take it. "We should order some Sharky's. I didn't eat dinner tonight, although I came close to eating. An amorous hipster smeared some food on my face and hands in a pathetic attempt at wooing me."

Harlow shakes her head and gets up to put the carton back in the freezer. "Um, ew." She sets down the carton. "I agree. If I keep eating this, I'll get sick. Order me a Caesar salad with dressing on the side while I change. Should we pick up or have it delivered?"

"Delivery," I say. "I'm not getting dressed again. It's pajama time for me."

"And then I'm gonna need to hear about these weirdos you picked up tonight," she says as she disappears down the hall and into her room.

I find the menu stuck to the side of our fridge with a magnet and call Sharky's, ordering her salad and a turkey avocado on a croissant for me. Harlow returns in her own sweats, hair piled into a wild and loose bun on top of her head, gorgeous green eyes now hidden behind the coke bottle lenses in her glasses.

"It'll be here in a half hour," I inform her as we sit back on the couch to kill some time.

"So your sister...Coral? How did you arrive at your conclusion about living life for her based on what happened to you tonight?"

"I don't know. I was one breath away from another panic attack all night long...and then I saw Grant. He was everything that was good and decent and stable in my life for a long time. Don't get me wrong, my parents are great, but he was the one I trusted above all others. Sadly, he's the one I treated the worst."

"Isn't that the way it always is?" Harlow asks, looking thoughtful. "There are times I want to kill my mom, but I'd kill for her, you know? We have the biggest fights sometimes but no matter what, she's the one who will always be there for me. I always call her first, good news, bad news, bad hair day, broken nail day. Whatever. She's my rock."

"I saw another guy tonight, another blast from the past. Oliver."

"Your midget boyfriend?"

"He's not an actual midget, and most midgets find that term incredibly insensitive."

She shrugs. "If it walks like a midget and talks like a midget..."

I throw a pillow at her to shut her up. "Oliver. He's fantastic. He was there too, trying to convince women like us to run away to join a circus with him, and they all took him seriously. Can you believe it?" I can't help laughing.

I sigh and keep going. "He had no idea what I'd done, what happened with Coral, or how I got so sick so fast. I pulled away from everyone and everything I cared about because I was worried I'd screw up, hurt them all again. I think seeing Grant was...I don't know...good for me. I needed to see him happy and successful. I know he's okay and he's moved on.

"But seeing Oliver...I think talking it out with

him got my brain working. I've known him longer than anyone else besides my family. He got me thinking of what I could do to honor the life of a girl much too young to die. I mean, what would my sister say if she saw me lying all stinky and depressed on the couch earlier tonight? I can almost hear her voice telling me to get up and get a life. Will it sound crazy if I say sometimes I feel like she's with me?" I look down and shake my head, my hands twitching nervously. "Maybe that's just me not wanting to let her go. I don't know, but she always looked up to me, for whatever reason. I don't want to disappoint her."

"So you have a plan? What is it?" Harlow asks quietly. I think she's afraid I might cry.

"First of all, you stop looking at me like I'm going to spontaneously combust, and we eat our take out."

She smiles ruefully at me. "Okay, and then what?"

"I find a job and do it well. Then I roll my parents into starting the Coral Brooks scholarship fund for foster girls, using the life insurance policy they had on her. What do you think?"

She nods approvingly. "I like it."

"My job hunting efforts have been a little lackluster, but—"

"A *little*? No kidding!" Harlow snorts.

I glare at her. "My plan doesn't require any commentary from you."

"And yet, you will hear it."

I laugh. "I know, I know..."

A knock at the door interrupts us a few minutes later as I finish fleshing out details for Harlow's opinion. "Hey, I got this one," I tell her as I reach for my purse on the table.

"You can barely pay rent right now," she protests, reaching for her own. "I got it." She hurries into the hall.

Johnny's business card falls out. "Hey, I forgot to tell you, I might have a temp gig to help me get rent money until..."

My voice trails off. My huge orange purse is loaded with a little too much stuff, but usually my wallet sits right on top, my life preserver floating atop a sea of worthless cosmetic flotsam. But it's not there. I start ripping frantically through my bag, looking for it. I throw out my phone, a notebook, pens in every shade, a few tampons, crinkled up receipts and gum wrappers. No wallet.

I dig through it again, checking for holes in the purse's lining. Harlow comes back to the table holding a plastic bag, loaded with two Styrofoam containers brim full with Sharky's deliciousness. "I can't find it!"

"Can't find what?" she asks, pulling out her salad. She slides the bag over to me and pops her container open to inspect the food.

"My wallet! I know I had it, I just..."

My voice trails off as I recall the last moment I saw Grant. I was so flustered that I knocked my purse to the floor and didn't bother making sure I had everything. I just grabbed what I could see and shoved it all back in so I could get out of there. "I left it at the coffee shop. Are they still open?"

We glance at the old analog clock ticking on the

wall above the table. Harlow pulls a face. "Sorry, but they closed an hour ago."

Of course. I guess it could be worse. It's not like I have much to lose in there. Any potential thief will be saddened by the serious lack of cash and credits cards that will most definitely get declined. It will probably end up in a trash can somewhere near the shop, but I still feel naked. Funny how all those official little papers and cards make me feel like someone.

I think hard. Maybe I dropped it in the front when I pulled my keys out to unlock the door? "I'll go look outside, just in case."

I head for the door, unlock everything, and step onto the patio, leaving it open so the light from the hall streams onto the small cement pad in front of our cute little garden apartment. A row of shrubs separates our courtyard from the neighbors, so l kneel down and reach into the foliage, shaking branches with the hope that my wallet will fall out like manna from heaven. The sky is an orange gray now that dark clouds have rolled in. I smell rain in the air. I'm crawling around on all fours, my hands getting scratched and shredded when my wallet magically appears before my eyes, floating right in front of me.

"What the...?" I fall onto my backside and sprawl out on the concrete. My head hits the base of the shrubs and what little long hair I have gets tangled with a sharp collection of twigs at the base, and all I can do is laugh. My eyes are cinched shut and I'm laughing like a maniac. Tonight starts with an eyeball guy and ends with me getting ambushed by a flying wallet and attacked by bushes. How much more bizarre can my life get at this point?

"Are you okay?" a very familiar and concerned voice asks.

Nothing surprises me more than that voice. "Grant?" I ask, sitting up. I think I leave a handful of hair behind in the bush as I lurch up in surprise, but I'm too shocked to feel it. "How did you find me?"

He squats down next to me and holds my wallet up. "You left this. I'm a creeper and went through it. Took your cash and went on a spending spree before I brought it back."

"With what I have in there? What did you buy, half a pack of gum?" I sit up and rub the back of my head, which is now pulsing with heat and pain. I touch it gently to feel the damage. I should have a lovely goose egg back there by morning.

"Oliver and I found it under the table where we sat tonight," he explains. Grant stands, offering a hand to help me up.

I sigh and take it, jumping lightly to my feet with his help. That jolt is back, the white hot burst of energy I feel when I see him and touch him. I stand there for just a moment, basking in it as light from the hall illuminates his perfect features, his hand still in mine. "Thanks," I murmur, working up the courage to look him in the eye. When my eyes reach his, I almost can't breathe. We stand there, hand in hand, for the longest moment, until a shadow blocks our light and I hear Harlow clearing her throat as discreetly as she can.

I look away. "Harlow, meet Grant. Grant, this is

my roommate Harlow."

She leans against the door frame and folds her arms, looking very much like a mother who just caught her kid smooching on the porch after curfew. "Grant, it's nice to meet you. I've heard absolutely nothing about you."

He grins and shakes his head, embarrassed. "Same here."

"He found my wallet at the coffee shop and was nice enough to bring it back to me," I tell her. I jump back and wipe the dirt and leaves from my backside. Coughing, I look down long enough to collect my thoughts, and then take the wallet from him. "Thanks again for bringing this by. You didn't have to go to the trouble."

"Hey, uh, Lauren," he starts, but he glances at Harlow, who's still standing in the doorway with an amused smirk on her face.

"Can I have a minute?" I ask her as my heart starts to beat foolishly in my chest.

Her eyes soften, and the porch light flips on as she closes the door. "You two crazy kids don't stay out too late," she says right before the door clicks shut.

Grant looks around, looking for a place to sit. We have nothing, unless he wants to use the shrubbery for a bench, so we stand in the odd yellow glimmer of the porch light. I'm so full of things I want to ask him, things I want to say, but that will take a lifetime, and I haven't earned it. Maybe he did walk away...but I'm the one who stayed away.

"So Oliver and I were talking," he begins, and his voice sounds a little high-pitched and unnatural. His nervous voice. I smile and fold my arms, tipping my head to listen. "We were wondering if you wanted to get together sometime for a casual dinner, you know, old friends just hanging out."

I offer an exaggerated nod. "Mm-hmm. You forget just how well I know Oliver. If I agree, he plans to come down with a mysterious case of food poisoning or leprosy that night and then experience a miraculous recovery next day, right?"

Grant's eyes close. "Something like that," he

admits with a half-smile.

"You brought me my wallet. Your good deed is done for the day," I say. I want to step away, but something draws me closer. "You've offered dinner with an old friend and I'd love to accept, but if I say yes, I don't want dinner with a friend."

"What are you saying?" He's closer now, too, and my face tilts up to search his even though it's partially hidden in shadow.

"I can't be friends with you, Grant."

He looks stunned and a little hurt. "What do you—"

Before I know what I'm doing, I move closer still and search his eyes. I may not know much, but I know I can't be just friends with him, ever. I need to see if it's still there, if he still wants me. I run my fingers through his thick curls and pull his head toward mine. My lips part and I feel the sweet warmth of his breath on my cheek before our lips meet. His hands cradle my face and then slide down my back as he pulls me closer. I taste the salt of his skin for a brief moment as I pull away, but he won't let me go. A light mist and gentle rain falls on us. It feels like time stands still as our hearts beat together and our lips meet again, soft and urgent, slow and deep, making promises we can't wait to keep. Our lips tell each other what we're not quite ready to say again. Not yet.

With a reluctant sigh, I pull away and look down. He keeps his hand on the back of my head, and pulls me into a hug. My head rests against his shoulder and he rubs my back slowly. "We can't pick up where we left off, Lauren."

"I don't want to," I answer as I wrap my arms around his waist. "I want something different. We aren't the same people we were five years ago. And you deserve so much more than I ever offered before."

"I wouldn't be here if I thought that," he whispers in my ear, his lips brushing it gently, the smell of him washing over me as I melt into him again. "You were always enough."

I don't know if I'm ready to believe in happily ever after yet, but I want to believe that we can be happy now. Maybe together we can recover the tomorrow we thought we lost, because, finally, my arms are wide open.

OTHER BOOKS BY JULI CALDWELL

PSYCHED

FREAKED

THE GATES OF ATLANTIS: SECRETS OF THE MINE

BEYOND PERFECTION

JULI CALDWELL

ABOUT THE AUTHOR

Juli Caldwell is a former columnist for Meridian Magazine, and has written dozens of guest articles for various literary and parenting publications. She holds a degree in English from Weber State University, with a minor in psychology. She lives in Utah with her husband, two children, and a dog who sheds too much. *Arms Wide Open* is her third book.

She blogs at julicaldwell.blogspot.com, and you can follow her on Twitter @ImJuliCaldwell or her Facebook page. Look for Juli Caldwell, Author.

If you liked this book, will you consider leaving it a review on Amazon or Goodreads? Authors depend on readers like you to share the word about books you love. Thank you!

Made in the USA
Lexington, KY
22 May 2015